PUFFIN BOOKS

DID YOU THINK I
LEAVE YOU CRYIN

CW00866975

A collection of stories w
different people – old and young – through the ages.
Quintus Maximus is a centurion in the XXth legion of
the Roman Army. Through his letters to his family we
learn what life was like on the march to fight the
Barbarians. Phil is a Falklands pilot, crazy about flying,
who doesn't want to talk about his experiences in the
War. Mike MacAllister is a ten-year-old boy who thinks
the German next door is a spy. Kevin and Margie find
friendship and warmth where they least expect it – and
they discover what (or who) is buried under the tree in
the old woman's garden.

A warm and sensitive collection – conflict, compassion,
friendship, heroism ... and the cruelty and futility of
war.

Moira Miller began writing scripts for the BBC's *Listen
with Mother* programmes. Her books include the 'Oh
Abigail' series which is dedicated to her daughter
Abigail and 'The Search for Spring' written for her son
Paul. *Did You Think I Would Leave You Crying?* is dedicated to her husband Louis. Her work as a storyteller in
schools and libraries throughout Scotland was well
known and her love of Celtic history lies behind much of
her writing. Moira Miller died in a road accident in April
1990. She was 49.

MOIRA MILLER

Did you think I would leave you crying?

PUFFIN BOOKS

PUFFIN BOOKS

Published by the Penguin Group
Penguin Books Ltd, 27 Wrights Lane, London w8 5tz, England
Viking Penguin, a division of Penguin Books USA Inc.
375 Hudson Street, New York, New York 10014, USA
Penguin Books Australia Ltd, Ringwood, Victoria, Australia
Penguin Books Canada Ltd, 2801 John Street, Markham, Ontario, Canada l3r 1b4
Penguin Books (NZ) Ltd, 182–190 Wairau Road, Auckland 10, New Zealand

Penguin Books Ltd, Registered Offices: Harmondsworth, Middlesex, England

First published by Methuen Children's Books Limited 1986
Published in Puffin Books 1991
10 9 8 7 6 5 4 3 2 1

Printed in England by Clays Ltd, St Ives plc

For Louis, with love

CONTENTS

TWO LITTLE BOYS

Two little boys had two little toys,
Each had a wooden horse.
Gaily they play, each summer's day,
Warriors both, of course.
One little chap then had a mishap,
Broke off his horse's head.
Wept for his toy, then cried with joy,
As his young playmate said:

'Did you think I would leave you crying
When there's room on my horse for two?
Climb up here, Jack, and don't be crying.
I can go just as fast with two.

When we grow up we'll both be soldiers,
And our horses will not be toys,
And I wonder if we'll remember,
When we were two little boys?'

PRELUDE

The Blade

Young Man woke early.

He woke like an animal, suddenly, quietly and with all his senses alive and aware. He lay at first with his eyes closed, holding his breath and listening. Whatever it was that had wakened him must have gone now. It might have been a marauding rat, scavenging the remains of last night's meal. It might have been a bird nesting, high in the dark, smoky roof of the cave. It might have been one of the dangerous prowling beasts foraging on the off-chance of finding them unguarded in the early morning.

Young Man raised himself on his elbow. In the dawn light the mouth of the cave showed as a faint grey hole, the walls lit by the dull red glow of the now dying Nightwatch Fire.

They were all safe. No beast would have passed the fire.

He lay down again on the skins and stretched out. The only sound to be heard now was the steady breathing of the Clan as they lay huddled around him on the sandy floor. He knew who and where they were just by listening.

Over to his right he heard the high whistling breath of the Old Woman. At his feet the soft grunting snore of Hunter, who spread out, large and powerful, across the cave mouth. Behind him the steady rhythm of Girl and her baby. There was only one baby now, the other one had died after the Wolf Attack.

Hunter had killed the Wolf himself, but too late.

Apart from them all, softly snoring on the white bearskin at the back of the cave was Chief. He stirred, moved stiffly, muttering something in his sleep. His hand, from long habit, held tightly to the Blade which already caught the dull gleam of the rising sun.

Young Man, moving silent as a cat, rolled over and came crouching to his feet. Holding his breath he slid round Hunter, keeping well back. Even a shadow falling on Hunter's eyelids was enough to bring him full awake. Young Man slipped out into the Dawn World.

Beneath him the Glen lay still and breathless. Mist spread thick along the river, lapping like a silent tide through the dark pines of the hillside. Here and there an early bird cried. High above on the mountain a beast roared, and defiance, fear or hatred echoed round the rocks. Young Man paused, frozen in his step; perhaps it was the beast that had awakened him. But it was far off, on the other side of the river perhaps, and no danger to the Clan.

Young Man breathed deeply and slowly. The air was clean, and already held the chill of the Cold Time that was coming. The smell was good, after the smoke and stench of the Living Cave. It was the smell of the High Mountain beyond the Glen, where already the snow lay in the top-most corries. Hunter had been there, during the long days of summer light. He had come back with deer and bear meat, and even Chief had not been able to provide so much food for the Clan.

Chief was becoming old, and since the Wolf Fight during the last Cold Time, he felt more pain. Young Man remembered when he and Hunter had been boy children and Chief had been the strongest creature in the Glen. He had brought food for them in plenty then, he and his brother Old Hunter. Together they had fought and hunted and fished the river. They had driven off Incomers from over the High Mountain. It was in one great fight that Old Hunter had died and Chief had taken the Blade from an Incomer.

That was a fight none of them would ever forget, with Chief and the Incomer roaring at each other like wild animals. They had fought on the stony shifting slope of the mountain, they had fought in the open by the Living Cave. There were times when it seemed that Chief must be destroyed by the flashing Blade, swifter and keener than a stone axe. But the Incomer, for all his skill with the Blade, was older and heavier, while Chief then was young and swift as a salmon twisting silver in the river.

In the end Incomer had died, and seeing in him a man of great strength and courage, Chief had his body laid on the Holy Stone by the waterfall. Then, in the hope that he too would be granted the same strength, the body was burned and the ashes used to draw a picture of the fight on the wall of the cave. Since that time Chief had slept beneath the picture with the Incomer's Blade, now his own, by his side. And so it had always been, except that now Chief was not so fast, and Hunter coveted the Blade.

Young Man stood up slowly, stretching to his full height. He was taller than Hunter now, though younger of course, and probably not as strong. One day he must test that strength as Hunter wanted to test his against Chief.

But not now. Not on this quiet morning with the sun beginning to warm the rock under his feet and the mist creeping off with the night, leaving the Glen river sparkling through the trees. Young Man lifted his short wooden fishing spear and the Killing Stone and loped off down through the trees.

The sun had almost reached the top of its Light Time when Young Man first heard the shouting. He lay on the grassy river bank, motionless, staring into the clear golden-brown water. In his hand the spear hovered, still as the kestrel high above the Glen, and every bit as deadly. In the shady ferns by his side lay five plump brown trout. A sixth nosed out from the overhanging bank beneath him into the sunlit current. Young Man held his breath, waiting his chance with the spear.

The shout broke through the silence of the golden morning.

Young Man, his whole being moving and thinking with the fish, heard nothing.

16

Another shout, followed by the wild high-pitched screaming of the Old Woman brought his head up. The trout, seeing the sudden shadow on the rocks, darted to safety in a flash of silver.

Young Man came to his feet, listening. The shouts came from the Living Cave. They came again, louder this time, calls of fear-hate from Man rather than wolf or bear. Leaving the fish where they lay, Young Man grabbed his Killing Stone and raced back up through the trees.

Was it a bear attacking the cave? Had Girl left the baby outside to be savaged by beast or bird? Had another Intruder found his way over the High Mountain? Or was it Hunter, claiming at last the Blade which he felt to be rightfully his?

As Young Man ran, fear siezed him. Chief was older and the wolf scars made him lame. He would fight using the Blade, with great cunning. But there was something in Hunter's head that was not in Young Man's or Chief's. Hunter had the way of the wild animals about him.

During the last Cold Time, Hunter would have killed Old Woman because she was an extra mouth to feed, and a useless one who could neither hunt nor bear children for the Clan. Chief had beaten Hunter then, beaten him to the ground and Old Woman, who, terrified, had crouched in the black depths of the Living Cave all the while, was left to help Girl with the babies, the cooking and the Fire-Which-Must-Never-Go-Out.

The shouts rang round the mountain-side again, echoing down the Glen as Young Man came out of the trees to see that his fears were right. Hunter and Chief fought as he had never seen them fight before.

Already both were bleeding heavily. The Blade swung, whistling round his head as Hunter, ducking and weaving, drove in with his great wooden spear. The spear that he had sharpened to a needle, hardened in the fire and stained with the blood of beast and man, swooped and stabbed. The Killing Stone in his other fist already ran with blood, his own and Chief's mingling.

They fought and fell, broke apart and came together again, circling each other with wary tread and watchful wolf-eyes. Old Woman crouched in the long grass, moaning softly, knowing already that the fight could only bring death, not only to Chief but to herself also.

Girl, clutching her baby, stood by the mouth of the Living Cave. Across the roaring, desperate fight she stared at Young Man and in her eyes he read the echo of his own fear. Not only the Blade, but she, too, would be Hunter's.

Fear turned to anger in Young Man. Girl had been promised to him, Chief had told him so, Girl wished it, and Hunter hated him for it. To win Girl, Hunter must kill him too, just as he was killing Chief, battering him to the ground with the Killing Stone.

Young Man howled in defiance, and stepped forward clutching his fishing spear and stone. Chief had fallen. Quickly, before Hunter could catch his wind and snatch the Blade, Young Man fell on him.

Hunter swung round, eyes blazing, teeth bared,

blood streaming from a Blade-cut on the side of his head. Young Man moved, swift, neat and very careful. Hunter was already exhausted, though still strong. In and out Young Man leapt, twisting and turning, forcing Hunter back and back towards the trees where his size and bulk and the long spear made the fight harder for him.

Back and forth they struggled. Hunter's Killing Stone caught Young Man across the chest. He heard Girl scream, but was hardly aware of the pain, his each sense tuned only to the attack. His whole mind concentrated on Hunter's every move, he waited for the mistake that would end the fight.

And at last it came. In his unthinking rage Hunter was drawn and lured towards the trees. He lunged furiously at Young Man's dancing feet. The long spear whipped through the air and caught in the tangle of brambles and undergrowth.

Only for a second, but it was enough. Young Man seized the chance, stepped in and drove his own short stabbing spear deep into Hunter's body. As the older man fell to the ground, Young Man hit him again and again with the Killing Stone.

Girl knelt in the crushed grass by the side of Chief. He opened his eyes as Young Man approached and saw the blood-stained spear and Killing Stone.

He smiled. His hand, holding the Blade, moved slowly towards Young Man and the fingers relaxed their grip. His eyes closed for ever as Young Man lifted the Blade and stood with the Girl in the golden sunlight.

In the sudden silence of the clearing the only sound to be heard was the voice of the Old Woman, crooning softly to the baby in the shelter of the Living Cave.

FUGUE

The Clasp

Quintus Maximus to his revered parents and family – Greetings

This letter comes late. I received your last only two days since. It has followed me from Deva through Luguvallium as we marched to the Northern Wall with the Legion. We were posted suddenly last month after weeks of fighting and rumour of more trouble amongst the barbarians beyond the Wall.

It seems that we are not to be here for too long. Thank the Gods for that. It is only a short time, but already I heartily loathe the place. Our commanders feel that the presence of the Legion alone should be enough to stamp out any further talk of rebellion. I hope they are right.

The few natives who live around the camp seem peaceful enough although they are a surly and unpleasant people, ignorant and silently hostile. Roman Law has taught them to be civilised; without it they are animals, but still they hate us.

This country of Caledonia is as cold and bleak as the people. We have all come to hate the endless hours of sentry duty, the constant wind and rain. One of our forts overlooks the River Clutha, the western end of our defences. On the very rare days when the weather is clear I can see our ships from the south lying at anchor or beached beneath the rock fortress that guards the channel. Some day I will leave on one of these ships. It cannot come too soon.

We all long for the off-duty spells when we can spend our time in the bathhouse down in the main camp. We talk, gamble and read letters from home. Marcus Antoninus – who sends his good wishes to my sister Petronia – says we sit on the bench in the Hot Room like the dried figs wrinkling in his father's loft.

How I think of you all around the table in the evening sun, reading this letter. I long to be with you, and send my love to my sisters and little brother, Julius.

Tell him if he would still join the Legions to beg the Emperor for a posting in the South. I cannot for the life of me imagine why we continue to occupy this forsaken land of cold and savages. There are those who have settled and built homes and farms in the south of Britannia, but surely no civilised man would choose to live in the North.

I would be grateful for another woollen cloak. At least then I may have one dry while the other steams with the loaves in the bakehouse.

With best wishes, love and respect from your loving son and brother.

Quintus Maximus

Quintus Maximus to his revered family – Greetings

Thank you for the cloak and letters with news of home, both most welcome.

Life here goes on as before, cold, dull and boring.

But great news. I have been appointed to lead a small detail on a mission beyond the Wall. Our Commander chose me himself, with some words which Father would have been proud to hear.

I can tell you little about the mission except that we are to meet and try to negotiate a peace with the leaders of some of the tribes from the mountains to the north of the Clutha. Very few of our own people have been to the mountains but we are to take with us a guide from one of the tribes who speaks a little of our language. I met him this morning. He has travelled far, living and eating like an animal. Marcus and the others are taking him to the bathhouse to clean and feed him and will bring him to my quarters later. I will leave this letter now and complete it when I am able to describe him to you more fully. It will amuse you.

My barbarian returned this evening. A strange young man, he is smaller than us with longer hair, brown in colour. His beard is a lighter red-gold. Most of his people stand before us with head bent, but not this man. He has a piercing stare that seems to see all at once. His eyes are not brown like ours but a curious grey or blue, the very colour almost of his own hills. He wears a rough brown cloak and a brightly coloured yellow tunic. You would have been most amazed, though, as I was, by the clasp of that cloak. It was of a soft grey metal and when fastened formed a cunningly wrought bird in a tree. I have never seen the like before. I asked him how he came by it, thinking it must have been stolen from some traveller. He said it was made by his own people and a gift from his father. I cannot believe these barbarians capable of such fine jewellery. I knew him to be a liar and told him so. He was angry but said nothing. They are cowards, these people, but all the same I shall take extra care to watch him on our journey north.

We leave tomorrow at first light. The northern hills which were lost in the mist a month ago are now clear and white with snow. I shall take both my warm cloaks. We also wear thick breeches against the cold and stuff our boots with rabbit fur. Marcus says we begin to look almost as wild as the natives. He also sends kind thanks to Petronia for her letter, but is writing to tell her so himself. We will now drink your health with some of his father's wine which arrived with the cloak.

Have no fears for our safety tomorrow. I have none myself, but trust in Mithras, the God of Soldiers.

With best wishes, much love and respect from your loving son and brother. I wish you good night.

Quintus Maximus

Marcus Antoninus to the Family of Quintus Maximus in haste and sorrow – Greetings.

I write at the request of Quintus Maximus. I know that he told you a little of our mission, but not of the dangers. He lies now in the camp hospital and has asked me to send on the enclosed package to you. It contains letters and papers written by him describing what happened, and a badge or insignia of some sort which he wished you to have.

There is little I can add for now. He is the best of leaders and fought with great courage. He brought us safely to within sight of the Wall but was severely wounded in a final attack. Few of us survived the mission, none are unhurt. The camp physician has been with him most of the day. I will sit with him tonight. With good fortune and prayer he may yet be well.

May his Gods grant him, and you, strength. I shall write further when there is more news, but be sure he is among good friends.

My love be with you all.   Marcus Antoninus

PAPERS ENCLOSED BY MARCUS ANTONINUS

Quintus Maximus to his revered parents and family – Greetings.

How strange it seems to write this with no way of knowing whether it may ever reach you.

We left camp, friends, the Northern Wall and the Empire behind us some seven days ago to set off into this waste of mountains.

We have brought with us a few pack-horses, but for the most part we travel on foot. The country is rough and we are all of us, although accustomed to long marches, completely exhausted. Only our guide seems not to notice how hard it is. He travels fast and lightly at the same steady pace and appears to need very little sleep, rest or food. He is not, of course, wearing full armour as we are, but carries only a short sword and a light spear.

He brought us at noon today to a village. The houses are low heaps of stone roofed with earth and from the hillside above were almost invisible. Only the smell of smoke and the barking of the wild hunting dogs which live with the people and fight constantly over scraps of food, told us where it was. The natives do not want us here. Our guide had to argue with them to force them to give us meat and shelter. The argument was long, and we could not understand any of it; they talk in a soft guttural tongue. They were unwilling to help, and hate us, but seem to have much respect for him.

He sleeps tonight in the main hut in a bed of furs while we share a pigsty floored and roofed with clods of earth. We ate together in the main hut, sitting on the floor around a smoking fire.

Perhaps it is true about the clasp on his cloak. The leader of the villagers brought out a wine cup, made of the same metal and curiously patterned and offered it to our guide. It seems to be their most prized possession.

Among these people this young man appears to have some power and be looked to as a leader. They treat him with respect and dignity which is strange in savages.

We have returned to our own hut to sleep now but can hear them singing. It is an eerie music, soft and sad like the wind. Marcus says that it reminds him of the pattern on the cloak clasp. I think I can understand what he means.

How we long to be back in camp with the bathhouse, clean clothes, wine and talk of home. Never has it seemed so far away.

We moved on from the village two days ago and have come at last to a hillside cave above a long narrow lake. Around us are high mountains as far as the eye can see. They are completely white against a sky that is as blue as the Adriatic on a summer day. I climbed to the top of this hill with our guide and he pointed out the pass where we will meet the tribal leaders. It as if the whole of Caledonia lay spread before us sparkling white with the rivers and lakes shining in the sun. It is a cruel but beautiful land.

From time to time as we travelled we have seen small groups of men on ponies who come out of the trees to watch us. Marcus said some at least had been at the village. He recognised a man with a scar on his leg. They must be following us.

This morning our guide spoke to the man. He

would not tell me what they said, but we knew it was a quarrel. Tonight, although it is bitterly cold they are still in the trees beneath the cave. Sometimes we see the glimmer of their fires, always we can hear their singing. Our men are coming to hate the sound. Some of them are frightened by it, although it is not warlike, but gentle and sad. I, too, feel uneasy.

Our guide came back from their camp tonight to tell us that tomorrow we will meet his people. Something is wrong. He, too, seems afraid or angry. When I ask him why, he pretends he does not understand me. I know he must.

All he will say is that we must march at daylight for the pass at the head of the lake. Now he sits outside the cave, wrapped in his cloak, staring at the blackness and the stars, while we huddle round the fire like so many mangy mongrels.

Mithras guide and guard us tonight.

It is now five days and nights since our meeting in the pass.

It was a trick, an ambush. These lying, thieving savages never had any intention of making peace.

There can never be peace. They wish only to drive us from their country. There can be no law when they say one thing, but lie and cheat and murder. Here there is only hate.

It happened suddenly. We filed up through the high rocky gully behind our guide. There was no one in sight and then every rock and tree was alive

30

with screaming, painted savages. We had no chance to form a square or shout orders. Each man fought for his own life.

But in that fight something happened. I cannot understand it, but neither can I forget it.

In the thick of the fight I felled a huge column of a man; anger must have given strength to my arm. I turned then to our guide, determined that I should be the one to run my sword through his lying, evil guts and found him beating down a savage who would surely have killed me.

He fought with incredible courage and in the end killed the man, but fell across me with a spear in his side. As we rolled over on the rocky slope he gripped the buckle of his cloak and held it towards me saying something in his own tongue. When he saw I could not understand he caught my hand in his and said it again in Latin.

'My father betrayed me. Take you this gift of a chieftain's son who would have made peace and lived with you in trust and honour.'

He died then with his strange blue eyes wide open staring at the sky. I cut the buckle from his cloak and kept it with me through the fighting. I have it with me still, as I can still see his eyes and feel the clasp of his hand.

A few of us were able to run from the pass and have come together again. Marcus, thank the Gods, is with us and safe. We must now try to find our way back to the Northern Wall. We hide by day and travel by night. Most of our armour which would betray us has been left behind. We carry only swords and a determination to win back and tell the others what has happened.

Tomorrow, perhaps, if I am right, we should be within sight of the Clutha.

If I do not return I have asked Marcus Antoninus to try to ensure that these papers and the cloak clasp are returned to you.

May our Gods grant us strength and courage, and may we meet again here or hereafter, in love and peace.

Quintus Maximus
Soldier of Imperial Rome
Centurion of the XXth Legion

SOLO

The Silver Bugle

There was once a young man called Iain who lived with his mother in a fishing village in the south of Scotland.

Iain passed his days working on the patch of land behind their grey stone cottage, or fishing with his neighbour Andrew who owned a small boat. In the evenings Iain would sit by the harbour chatting with the other men or strolling over the grassy headland above the village with Andrew's sister Rose. He and Rose had grown up and gone to school together and he could not remember a time when he had not loved her dearly.

It had long been agreed that one day they would marry, and indeed Andrew and Iain's mother would have liked nothing better.

'But not yet awhile,' said Iain. 'I'm too young to marry yet. I want to get away from the village to see the world first.'

'I'm sure I don't know where you get these daft-like notions,' grumbled his mother shaking her head. 'There's nothing better than your own fireside, and that's a fact.'

But however much she grumbled, Iain was still unsettled and spent his days and nights dreaming about far-off places and grand adventures. So he might have gone on, dreaming only, had it not been for the Stranger.

He arrived in the village one afternoon in the early spring, just about the time of year when the cuckoo returns from a winter spent in warmer countries far to the south. The Stranger came swinging along the high road and a fine sight he made in his old red army coat with a battered silver bugle slung on a leather strap across his chest. He was a big man with a rich voice and a rare gift for storytelling. And what stories he had to tell.

He sat on a bench outside the Inn spinning tales for anyone who stopped to listen. He spoke of his adventures with the King's army in countries across the sea where the people knew only strange words that made little sense to man nor beast; he spoke of countries where the sun shone all the year long, and where the flowers grew, even in the winter-time.

'Flowers in the winter-time! Whoever heard such-like nonsense,' said Iain's mother. She had stopped on her way back from the shop to listen to some of the stories. She sniffed, pulled her shawl around her and stumped off home again, calling to Iain to follow her.

But Iain heard not a word she said. He sat at the Stranger's feet, spellbound. Andrew came to ask if he would go fishing but Iain waved him away. Even Rose could only stand and watch as Iain hung, enchanted, on every word the Stranger spoke. Gradually, as evening came on, the village people drifted off to their homes, leaving Iain and the

Stranger alone. At last the Stranger fell silent, as together they sat gazing out across the darkening sea towards the setting sun, each thinking his own thoughts.

Iain stretched and yawned.

'Time for home,' he said. And then he saw that in the dying rays of the sun the man's coat seemed a brighter red and the polished metal of the old battered bugle flashed and sparked like fire.

'It's a bonny wee trumpet that,' he whispered running a finger along the cold metal. 'I'd like fine to hear it, just the once.'

The Stranger smiled, lifted the bugle to his lips and blew five strong notes that rang out across the village until the very walls seemed to answer back. The notes echoed in Iain's heart and blood like a call that he had been awaiting all his life.

'Can I do it?' he asked, breathless with excitement. The man laughed and handed him the bugle, showing him how to hold it and blow the notes. Iain blew clear and true as the sun dipped slowly into the sea.

'Aye, you'd make a right fine soldier, son,' said the man. 'Here, you keep the bugle. It came from a young man just like you, and he'll not be wanting it now.'

Iain lay in bed with the bugle by his pillow. All night long he tossed and turned, unable to sleep, his head full of uniforms and drums, trumpets and banners. By the morning he had made up his mind what he must do.

He packed his few belongings into an old leather

37

pouch and told his mother he was off to Edinburgh to join the King's Army.

'I kent it,' she wailed. 'You'll be killed, and what about me? What about your old mother. . . .'

'Och, mother!' said Iain. 'Rose and Andrew will be here to help. I'll not be killed. I'll be back soon with medals and silver in my purse. You'll see.'

Rose was in the garden at the back of the cottage hanging out the washing as he left. She cried and begged him to stay. But Iain had the sound of a silver bugle, and dreams of a fine red coat before him. He kissed her on the tip of her freckled nose, said goodbye, and set off up the hill to the High Road.

At the top he turned and looked back. The wee village had never looked so bonny. The long winter had finally passed, leaving behind a carpet of sweet new grass and trees uncurling into pale green leaf. From where he stood he could still see Rose, pinning out the washing, her red hair tossing in the fresh west wind that blew in from the sea. Somewhere up the hill a new-born lamb bleated for his mother, and from the woods behind him a cuckoo called. Over and over again.

Iain was filled with delight. He lifted the silver bugle to his lips and blew two long notes in answer. That was how he left the village, stepping out along the High Road, singing, with his fine silver bugle by his side.

He marched for days along dusty roads, past cottages and farms, through towns and villages, until at last he came to the great bustling city of Edinburgh.

Iain had never seen anything like it before. He stood and gawped in wonder as people pushed and jostled in the narrow streets. Tall buildings crammed together, as though all trying to stand on the same spot at once, fighting to see which could get closest to the great grey castle on the cliff-top.

In the little streets around their feet were market stalls, shops full of fruit and vegetables, baskets of fish and rolls of cloth, all colours of the rainbow, and over everything, the shouting and bustle of hundreds of folk buying and selling.

'My, I wish Rose was here to see all this,' thought Iain. But the idea was no sooner in his head than it was pushed out again.

There came the rattle of a drum, the ring of a bugle, a shout from the dirty children playing in the gutter and the next minute Iain felt himself pulled along with the crowds as they swept forward to catch a glimpse of a regiment of soldiers as they marched up the cobbled street to the castle.

Oh, the glitter of those swords in the sunlight, the red coats, the stamp of boots on the stones! At the head of them all, filled with all the pride in Edinburgh Town, marched a boy with a bugle. He stepped proud and stiff, blowing as if he would tell the whole world to make way.

Iain pushed and shoved through the crowds and fell into step behind the soldiers, marching right up the hill into the castle.

And so it was he came to join the King's Army.

They gave him a red coat, and taught him how to blow his bugle so that the soldiers would march to his tune. And did he not wish that his mother and Rose and Andrew – and indeed the whole village – might have been there to see him marching up the hill in front of his regiment.

Time passed and at long last Iain's regiment was sent to fight for the King in foreign lands. Across the sea in stormy autumn gales they went. Many were sick, but Iain was a good sailor and spent his time on deck, watching for his first sight of the wonderful lands the Stranger had promised him, the lands where the sun shone all day and the flowers grew, even in winter-time.

But it was not to be like that.

Everywhere they went the land was grey and muddy. They marched for days on end through little villages which must at one time have looked much like his own. Now, though, the trim gardens were trampled, the houses burned and farms deserted and weed-grown.

One time they came across the ruins of a deserted village. In the fields around, where once the corn would have grown rich and golden, were only scattered make-shift crosses. In the empty church, roof open to the sky, Iain found the name of the village and remembered it as a great battle that the King's Army had won a year ago.

Again they marched on, and as they marched it rained until their fine red coats were covered in mud and the swords lay rusting in their sheaths. Even the silver bugle grew dull and dirty, although Iain would sit and polish it whenever they stopped for a rest.

There were times when a party of soldiers scouting ahead came across a group of the enemy hiding in a lonely farm or wood, and then there was a skirmish, brief and bloody, with men hitting out blindly at each other in panic.

But after all they would march forward, on and on down the endless muddy roads.

Autumn drew into winter as the army marched further south, and found them in the mountains, where the snow lay in the high valleys all year round. The cold ate right through the old red coats, into their very bones. It seemed to Iain that even if he put his hands into the heart of the campfire flames they would never feel the heat again. As winter straggled into sodden, chilling spring the snows thawed and the army moved down through the high mountain passes into the valleys below.

It happened that one day Iain was sent on ahead with a small group of men to search out a camp for the night. Down through the trees they slithered and stumbled to a place where a tumbling mountain burn widened into a deep brown pool. The water slid like silk over the smooth stones, and above their heads, among the plump buds of spring, birds sang in the first sunlight they had seen for many a long and weary day.

Iain and the others fell on the soft grass by the pool, exhausted, tattered and hungry, and in the peace of the gentle place they fell asleep.

An hour passed, or maybe two; men slept and

dreamt, and turning, slept again. The afternoon stretched out, slow and warm and sleepy.

Then suddenly the peace and silence were shattered. Birds flew screaming from the trees. A scavenging party of enemy soldiers fell upon them.

Iain leapt to his feet, reaching for the bugle to sound the alarm and was felled by a blow from behind.

They found him, many hours later, by the tumbling waters of the burn, still holding tightly to the silver bugle. He stirred as they moved him, and felt himself lifted gently and wrapped in a rough woollen blanket. From far and high above there came voices.

'Aye, careful here.'

'The wee lad's hurt gey bad, I'm thinking.'

'Move him easy there.'

'. . . into the sun. . . he's no' long. . . .'

And indeed Iain felt himself slipping slowly away from them. The voices and the sound of the river wove together, fading gradually. The pain and cold had long since left him and he lay floating as if in some silver mist.

And then at once there came another sound, cutting across the rest, clean and pure.

Cuckoo, cuckoo!

The little bird, that like himself had spent the winter in foreign lands, was now preparing to return home to Scotland.

Iain saw again in his mind's eye the wee village. Rose in the garden with her fine red hair, braver than any army coat, the washing streaming like a banner in the west wind. He saw the glittering sea, brighter than any bugle.

With a great effort he pulled himself up on to one elbow. He lifted the silver bugle to his lips and blew with all the breath left in his body. He blew two long clear notes in answer to the little brown cuckoo-bird that had followed him so far.

And his call rang out, sharp and clean and echoing round the quiet glen.

'I'm coming home,' it said. 'I'm coming home.'

Home to Rose, and the wee grey cottage by the beach. Home to his mother, and Andrew and the boat. Home to his own green hillside and the little wood where the new leaves shimmered in the sunshine, and the cuckoo sang for the sheer joy of another spring.

DUET

Old Bandy and Rapunzel

Growing up is a funny thing. It can be so slow sometimes that you begin to wonder if it will ever happen. You seem to be hanging around waiting for it forever.

'No, you can't go out on your own. Wait till you're grown up. . . .'

'I want you back in by ten o'clock. You can do what you like when you're grown up. . . .'

Other times growing up happens all of a heap, when you least expect it. And it takes a long time before you realise that's what it actually was anyway. It doesn't feel the way you thought it would.

Once upon a time – I know that's a pretty wet way to start a story but it really was like that – anyway once upon a time, light-years ago I was ten years old, at Primary School. I was a round, fat pudding with thin stringy hair. The one in the photograph with the wrong coloured socks and the tie not properly fastened up – that's me.

Next to me you'd see Morag, neat and tidy with her hair beautifully tied up in two thick pigtails. Standing behind Morag – and tying her pigtails together – would be Mike. The three of us lived in the same street, played in each other's gardens, and

47

shared the same Air Raid Shelter on the bad nights. It was a bit of a squeeze what with Morag's Grandad and three Mums as well. No Dads though, there were very few Dads around at that time, they were all out winning the War for us at home.

It was up on the flat roof of the shelter one day during the summer holidays that it all started. Mike and Morag had joined me and we were all a bit fed up. It was the sort of day that's so hot even the birds have gone to sleep, so quiet you could hear the machinery and men shouting to each other in the dockyard down the hill.

Mike stood up on tiptoe. He was beginning to grow really tall, just like his dad, and his short grey trousers looked a bit silly on the long stringy legs.

'You can see everything they're doing from up here,' he shouted. 'They're repairing that corvette that came in last week, and the minesweeper looks as if it's ready to go back out again.'

'Keep your voice down,' I hissed. 'My mum says, "Walls have ears." There could be a German spy listening to anything you're saying.' A German Spy was just about the worst thing you could possibly think of just then.

Morag giggled. I had to admit the idea of a spy in our quiet little seaside town was a bit odd. Anyone who was in the least bit different was immediately noticed and gossiped about down at the shops. My dad always said Mrs Jack at the Dairy ran the best Intelligence Network in the country!

Anyway, Mike was standing there in the sunshine, slowly turning like the look-out sentry at the yard, when he suddenly stopped and sat down with a thump.

'Watch it!' I shouted. He landed on top of me.

'Shhhhhh,' he put his hand over my mouth. 'There *is* a spy.'

'Rubbish!' I said sitting up and trying to bite his finger. Well, you wouldn't have liked it either. His hands were filthy. Mike said nothing, just nodded in the direction of the house that stood back to back with ours.

'Old Bandy,' I said. 'You must be joking. He's harmless.'

'He's at the attic window,' hissed Mike, climbing up on to his knees to look again. 'And he's watching the yard.'

'He's a foreigner,' Morag whispered in dramatic horror. 'He speaks *German*. My mum said when he moved in there were boxes of German books in the front garden. She says. . . .'

'Doesn't make him a spy,' I said. 'Besides he's *ancient* and he can't speak English very well.'

'He's probably a master of disguise,' said Mike. He had completely convinced himself by now that Old Bandy was dangerous. 'It's a white wig and a cushion stuffed up his front.' Mike read far too many comics. There was no talking him out of it, and by the time he'd finished he had Morag and even me half convinced that Old Bandy must be a spy.

'I bet They sent him to keep an eye on the yard. We'll keep a check on his movements and notify the

Police.' Mike had gone all important. I could just see him inventing the headlines:

'SCHOOLBOY SAVES COUNTRY – GEORGE MEDAL AWARDED TO MICHAEL MACALLISTER'

'. . . . are you listening?' He poked me in the ribs. 'You live nearest so you can keep an eye open at night and take a note of anything strange.'

I thought it was nonsense. Old Bandy had lived back to back with us for years and nobody ever saw him. Not surprising really, he'd never cut the hedge or trimmed the roses in all that time.

It didn't seem such nonsense later on that night, though. Funny how things are never quite the same in the dark. I was quite late going to bed. We'd all been listening to a Variety Show on the wireless and when I did go Mum shouted through to me not to read in bed so I said 'OK' and sneaked my torch up with me.

I always read in bed, with the light on when it's all right, and under the covers with a torch when it's not. I had this book I kept hidden under the mattress and I only read it when I was on my own in bed. No, it wasn't the kind of book you're thinking. We'd looked at the pictures in the Medical Book Morag's mum had. It was nothing like that.

It was worse in a way because it was German.

I'd found it right at the bottom of a heap of mouldy old books when I was helping my gran to clear out the cupboard in the kitchen. It was a right mess with the covers falling off and pages crumpled.

There was a name written inside in funny old scratchy letters, as if a spider had stepped in ink and staggered across the page. It was probably even more ancient than Old Bandy if that was possible.

When I looked inside, it had these amazing pictures, all black and white with castles and horrible gnomes and spiky trees. The stories were written by two brothers called Jacob and Wilhelm Grimm. There was a picture of them at the front which was pretty dreadful, too.

'Nasty thing,' said my gran. 'Germans. Never did like that book. Throw it away.'

But I didn't. I stuffed it in my schoolbag to take home and read. I suppose in a way that was the first part of growing up. Usually I'd have done exactly what she said.

Anyway, I had the book at home and I kept it under the mattress, right in the middle where Mum wouldn't find it. Not even when she was making the bed. Every night I jammed a chair in front of the bedroom door so that I would have time to hide it if anyone tried to come in.

The stories were wonderful. It was annoying, though, that I couldn't tell Morag or Mike. Nobody could know that I was reading a *German* book. It was probably treason or something like that.

Anyway that night I was reading one called 'Rapunzel' about a princess who was kept prisoner in a tower in the Wild Wood by an evil old witch. The picture was really horrible with brambles and thorns around the tower, a bit like Old Bandy's garden. Right at the top at a tiny window, sat the princess bewailing her fate and at the bottom among the thorns was a horrible witch and hundreds of evil creatures like little devils. It was really gruesome that picture, it made me want to cry, and the story wasn't much better. I knew as soon as I switched off the torch I was going to have nightmares, so I tried to think of something else to do before going to sleep, and I remembered Old Bandy.

I switched off the torch, tiptoed to the window and pulled back the blackout curtain. We have to have curtains like that so as not to show any lights for the German bombers. It was very late but because it was summer the sky was still not quite dark.

I could see over the wall into Old Bandy's garden. There was something moving under the trees. A flash of white and I knew it was Old Bandy's hair. He was creeping about in the bushes! I watched for ages to see what he was up to but it was getting darker and in the end I had to give up. Mike was right, though. He *was* up to something.

Every night after that I watched and it was always the same. Late on, once it began to get dark Old Bandy would come out into the garden and walk around, never in the middle, always under the trees as if he was hiding something. He walked round and round. It was really weird.

Soon I began to find that I was watching for him all the time. I couldn't get him out of my head, somehow. He went round and round like he did in the garden. I asked Mum about him, but she didn't know – or wouldn't say – much. She thought he'd come from Germany at the beginning of the War and some people said he used to be a schoolteacher, but she didn't want to talk about it. When I went on asking questions she told me to stop being silly.

I watched all the time after that. He never came out into the wild garden during the day, but stood at the attic window for hours on end just staring. It was only at night he came out to creep around like an old badger.

I started going to school the long way round and peering through his front gate, and spent hours sitting on top of the shelter that summer watching for something to happen – but it never did.

The garden grew wilder and the hedge thickened up with the roses tangled through it. The only person who went in was an old cleaning lady who took his shopping twice a week. Mrs Jack down at the shop tried to find out what he was doing, but the cleaning lady had no idea. She never saw him; he stayed up in the attic while she was in the house.

It was very, very peculiar. Rather like the stories in the Grimm book that I couldn't tell anyone about.

Finally, I told Mike about Old Bandy but by that time he had lost interest. He was always keener on the ships down the yard anyway, or playing football, or maybe it was because I was the only one who ever saw anything and that annoyed him. Anyway he gave up spy-hunting.

'He's mad,' he said. 'Just a daft old codger.' Morag wasn't bothered either way, she never was about most things. But I was really curious by this time, and I knew by then that he knew I was watching him.

We would stand and stare at each other for ages. I never waved, and neither did he. I don't know why. It just didn't seem right, somehow.

It could have gone on like that I suppose, but for one Saturday afternoon when I was sitting on the shelter. Morag had gone shopping with her mum and Mike was at a football match. I concentrated my eyes into pin pricks and stared hard at the attic window. There was this character in one of Mike's comics who could make people do what he wanted by the power of his hypnotic eyes. I had to try it out myself.

'Come to the window,' I willed inside my head. 'Come to the window.'

It was terrifying. He not only came, he stood there and stared straight back at me! And then he lifted a long white finger – and beckoned to me to come over.

I didn't believe it! I just stood there on the shelter roof hoping I was invisible or something stupid, but it only happens like that in Grimm's stories. It was me he was looking at and waving to.

Of course I knew I shouldn't go. My mum would have had a fit if I had asked her, but she was busy in the front room with the sewing machine, and somehow I couldn't stop myself. It was as if *he* was the wizard and had put a hypnotic spell on me.

It wasn't easy getting there. The briar roses tangled round the latch on his front gate like barbed wire. I had fought my way up the front path through the jungle and was ringing the bell before I suddenly realised that nobody knew I was going there. What if something awful happened?

I was just about to turn and run when it did.

The front door opened, just a crack, and there stood Old Bandy, the first time I had ever seen him close-to. That was a surprise for a start. He was smaller than I had imagined, like a little gnome, and he looked so old. I always thought Grannie was the oldest person in the world, but Old Bandy's face was covered in tiny crinkly lines and the skin was white like paper. We stood and stared at each other, it seemed like forever, before he spoke.

'Why you watch me?' he said. 'Always you watch, watch, watch.' His voice was exactly like a German Spy in a film, but old and wavery.

I couldn't think what to say. I shook my head.

'Always the same. Out of my window I see you. Watch, watch, watch. You want to see what my house looks like inside? Come in.' He stepped back and held open the door. I don't know why, I walked into the hall. He closed the front door behind me and held out a hand.

'How do you do? Now you are come to visit.'

I shook hands with him and nearly screamed. You could feel the bones right through the skin, like a bird's claw.

'Please this way?' He waved to me to walk into the big room off the hall. It was like being in a dream where everything was real, but not quite real, if you know what I mean.

'Wait,' he said and went out leaving me on my own. It was awful. The room was full of old dark furniture, and I could hear the whole house being quiet around me. the smell was like the inside of my grannie's wardrobe – stuffy and warm. In the middle of the floor stood a small table with curly legs and horrible claw feet that held on to wooden balls. It reminded me of the handshake. There was a saggy leather armchair by the fire with Old Bandy's shape pressed into the back and seat as if a ghost was sitting there.

'Frightful things!' he said. He had crept back into the room behind me. I nearly jumped a foot in the air, I hadn't heard him. He put a tea-tray down on the table and waved a hand around.

'Frightful things, the furniture, but not mine. All I have is my books.' There was a little bookcase beside the big chair.

'All mine,' he said stroking them. 'These they did not burn.'

I went over to look at the books. I thought it was only polite although I knew they wouldn't mean a thing to me. He picked out an old red-leathered covered one and opened it.

There was the same picture!

'Jacob and Wilhelm Grimm!' I gasped before I could stop myself. Suddenly his ancient crinkly face lit up and cracked into a sort of smile. It was like the stories, half-horrible, half-fascinating.

'You know!' he nodded. 'Is good. Is very good.'

'Rapunzel,' I said. 'Hansel and Gretel!'

'Ja . . . ja . . . ' he nodded. I watched his old fingers, like thin white sticks turn the pages, stopping at the pictures which were exactly the same as the ones in my book. On one page a child had drawn a funny little frog at the end of a story. He smiled again and shook his head. His eyes were strange as if he was a long way off and looking at something quite different. And still he went on turning and turning the pages.

'What do you look for?' I don't know what made me say it, or why, I only knew I was no longer afraid of him. He turned slowly and stared at me, as if he had forgotten I was there.

'Every night, in the garden . . . what are you looking for?' He glanced quickly around the room as if somebody might be listening.

'I go for walk,' he whispered. He was so close I could smell his fusty old jacket.

'In the dark?'

'Always I go in the dark.'

'But why not during the day?' I said. 'You can't see anything at night.'

'Cannot *be* seen,' he said. 'Three years I must hide after they take. . . .'

' . . . who?' I know it was rude. Grannie would have told me to mind my own business, but I felt as if it was very important. I had to know.

He stopped suddenly and stared at me. His old eyes were like pale blue glass marbles, shining and silvery. I had the feeling he couldn't see me again. He was talking to somebody else.

'I must not go out,' he said. 'They will come for

me too!' He went over and closed the curtains. Pulled them shut on the sun outside, and sat huddled in the big armchair. I left him like that and slipped back to my own garden. It felt as if I had been away for hours, but nobody had noticed. It was like one of these stories where magic makes time stop.

I didn't really understand then, except that something horrific had happened. Something so appalling that everyone had to fight it, but no one could really stop it. Not the ships in the dockyard or my dad in the army or Morag's or even Mike's.

I never told them about the visit, or my mum either. Old Bandy went on staring out of his window day after day, not at the dockyard, but across a cold grey North Sea and into a past that held unimaginable terrors. I never went back to visit him because he died not long after that, still trapped in his own prison behind the wild garden. They had to chop down the thorns and drag away the brambles to carry his coffin out into the sunshine of the cemetery.

I think that was when I began to grow up.

The Grimm book stayed under the mattress for ages. Much later I found out that Mum knew about it all the time and just left it. It was so old that it fell apart in the end, but I kept the pages together in a shoe box. They're still there now, all except the picture of Rapunzel.

I framed that and it hangs above my bed. It's ancient, brown and spotty, but the princess still stands in her high tower searching for a rescuer while the witch and her evil creatures dance among the thorns.

And it still makes me cry.

TRIO

Per Ardua . . .

Pop pulled into the layby at the top of the hill, turned off the ignition and wound down the window. Beneath them, the rich farmland of Moray lay spread out like a glorious green and brown carpet sweeping down to an unexpectedly Mediterranean blue firth.

'Aye – spring's back,' he said. 'No two ways about it.'

Lorna slid down in the passenger seat of her grandfather's old Jaguar, stretched out her legs and breathed deeply. It was spring all right. You could smell the fresh wet earth of the newly ploughed fields and the sea, clean and sharp in the breeze. If you closed your eyes and concentrated really hard you could pick up that other magical smell, the paraffin whiff of aviation fuel drifting across from the new airfield down by the lighthouse. Funny how they always called it the new airfield, thought Lorna. It had been built way before the Second War, at the time the old First War airfield was closed down.

Pop scratched a light and puffed quietly at his pipe. Sweet aromatic scent drifted in to join the other smells. Lorna breathed deeply, savouring the feel of hot leather seats and the pipe tobacco that had been part of so many weekends spent with her grandfather, sometimes walking, sometimes shopping, sometimes, as today, going fishing. Every Saturday of her life almost. How many was that? Her brain ticked over slowly in the sleepy heat.

Thirteen times fifty-two, add Christmases and New Years, when Pop always came over and spent four days with them, take away the time she had measles and the chickenpox fortnight . . . and what about Leap Years, did they happen at weekends? Lorna's mind slid into a dozy trance, playing with the numbers. If she turned her face to the sun she could see them floating against the bright pink of her closed eyelids. Like alphabet soup, she thought, where you always felt the words would make sense if you could just find which was the first letter. . . .

The drone of the Spitfire engine cut a sharp slice through her dream.

'Phil's back,' chuckled Pop. Lorna sat up suddenly and opened her eyes. Dazzled at first by the sun she missed the little plane, and then suddenly she saw it come swooping and banking over the dark band of pine trees around the old airfield.

'Fantastic,' she breathed as the Spitfire lifted against the blue sky, and turning, seemed to hang motionless in the air before swooping into a power dive. Pop nodded and watched with nostalgic pleasure as the plane levelled off and headed out over the fields for another circuit.

'Let's go down and meet him,' said Lorna

bouncing round in her seat. Pop smiled. He already had the engine started and was sliding off down the road.

Phil saw them and waved as the car turned into the gateway of the deserted airfield. It bounced down the cracked concrete to the abandoned hangars which he and the others used as a temporary flying club.

'What-ho!' he shouted, looking up briefly from the remote control unit. The tiny Spitfire dipped dangerously, then just as quickly levelled out as Phil regained control. She banked into a Victory Roll in front of the empty sheds and bounced down the split and weed-grown runway to stop in front of Phil as Pop's car pulled up behind him.

'Not bad!' said Pop laughing. 'You've been practising on holiday.'

'It's a new one!' shouted Lorna tumbling out of the car. 'You've bought a new Spitfire. That's a Mark 9, *and* you've got a new control unit.'

'Very good,' said Phil. 'Later model. Decided it was time we up-dated the Squadron. What do you think, Wingco?' He always referred to Pop as the Wing Commander although he had never been more than a Flight Sergeant during the war. Technically, as Flying Officer, Phil would have been his senior, but it never seemed like that.

Pop smiled. 'She's a wee cracker, right enough,' he said, inspecting the little plane more closely.

'Bet it was fast,' said Lorna. 'The real one, I mean.'

'Faster than the Messerschmidts, anyway,' said Phil. His enthusiasm for, and knowlege of Second War aircraft, was every bit as keen as hers.

'You flew a Mark 9, Pop, didn't you? There's photos of them in your scrapbook.'

'When was that, then?' said Phil. But Pop was not to be drawn.

'I was only a stoker on the coal-fired ones.' He paused to relight his pipe as he strolled back to the car. 'Anyone fancy a coffee? We *were* going fishing. I brought a flask with me.'

It was always like that with her grandfather, thought Lorna, irritated. Every time you tried to get him to talk about something really interesting – about the years he spent flying during the War, he just changed the subject, or made a joke about it – or both. He never stopped and talked about things the way Phil did. Phil looked funny, with that fluffy ginger moustache and his permanently-planning-a-practical-joke expression, but he would sit and chat for hours on end about flying and what it felt like, and about the War, which fascinated him just as much as it did Lorna.

They had met him quite by accident. Phil had crashed an early Spitfire down by the river bank one Saturday afternoon when she and Pop were fishing. At least Pop was fishing; Lorna had caught nothing but a pair of very wet socks. She abandoned the rod and helped Phil search, finally unearthing the plane in a clump of nettles.

'Wizard prang!' said Phil, laying on the Biggles voice thick. 'Enemy territory, what?' Together they used the butt of her rod to pull the little aircraft clear.

'. . . and without getting stung once,' said Phil. 'Worth a D.F.C. that is.'

'Pop's got one of these,' said Lorna. 'He's my grandad.' From then on a firm friendship had grown. Pop brewed a pot of tea on the camping stove, Phil split his Mars Bar three ways, and in no time they were talking flying. At least Phil and Lorna were. Pop as always refused to be serious about it.

And he still refused to be serious, sharing a coffee over Phil's new Spitfire.

'Time I was back,' said Phil at last. As they helped him pack the plane into the impossibly small back seat of his little white sports car Pop picked up an old newspaper. The huge black headlines were shouting the same message as the radio and television had for days past.

'What about this Falklands thing?' he said. 'Think it'll come to anything?'

'Lord knows,' said Phil. 'Hard to tell what's going on. As long as they don't leave us out of it. If there's fun and games going I want to be in on it!' He tossed the paper into the back of the car, climbed in and revved into a racing start down the runway. A wave of his hand, a flash of sunlight on the ginger-blond hair and Phil had gone, leaving them standing on the deserted airfield.

A cloud slid across the sun. Lorna shivered suddenly aware of the sea wind, still cold and icy in the early spring. Pop smiled and shook his head.

'Idiot,' he said quietly.

The white sports car roared off down the long straight road to the new airfield, the engine fading until it sounded exactly like the model plane.

There was no sign of Phil at the old airfield the week after that, nor the following week. Indeed there were very few model planes flying, and Dodge Foster in Lorna's class, whose dad was a painter, said that the Squadron had been called south.

'How do *you* know?' said Lorna. Dodge's head was normally full of pop music and break dancing. He wouldn't have noticed a plane if it had landed in his porridge.

''S'true,' Dodge insisted. 'My dad's working at the base just now. He says half of them have gone.'

'Think he's been sent to the Falklands?' she asked Pop. But Pop only shook his head, without looking up from the paper. The Falklands was getting serious now, with talk of real trouble.

'No idea,' he said. Lorna watched every news story on television in case there was a glimpse of Phil going south with the Task Force or with the R.A.F. on Ascension Island, but she never saw him.

The weeks went by and the news became worse and worse. At first it had seemed like fun, a great adventure, but then a ship was sunk – one of theirs – and the whole thing began to seem much more frightening.

One night Lorna came home from dancing class

to find everyone staring silently at the television set and the man from the Defence Ministry with the voice like a speaking clock talking of 'one of our ships being sunk' and 'unknown casualties'. She ran up to her bedroom and slammed the door, trying to blot out the voice, but it was still there in the corner of her own comfortable home, talking about death and drowning. The pictures merged together in her mind with the laughing faces and jokes of the men who had gone with the Task Force.

'No, no, no!' she screamed in the silence inside her head. She threw her shoes at the wall and fell on the bed burying her face in the pillow, but the faces were still there.

Above her head the photographs and posters of aircraft Phil had given her roared in silent fly-past.

'What'll happen?' she asked Pop time and again. 'Will Phil be all right?' The stories of planes shot down and pilots lost were growing daily.

'He can look after himself, lass,' said Pop quietly. 'That's what he's been trained to do. It's up to him – and the lads he works with – they know what they're doing. He'll get back – if he's there. We don't even know he's gone, remember?'

But somehow Lorna felt sure that Phil was there, in among the fighting and the mud and the cold of the South Atlantic. She sat glued to the television night after night, watching every news bulletin, studying the faces in the crowds. There was one time when she caught a glimpse of a ginger-blond head above a combat jacket.

Phil would not have been wearing a combat

jacket, though, and when he turned the man was older and thinner, with no moustache.

The weeks dragged on with losses and gains. Goose Green was taken back, but men died. A troop ship full of soldiers was hit, so close inshore it looked as if they could have swum to safety, but men died. The final attack was made, and Port Stanley recaptured, and still more men died on the bleak islands.

Lorna sat horrified as Pop watched, in tears, the church service from Stanley Cathedral. Rows of burly young men, dirty and tired, in muddy battle dress, some of them singing a quiet hymn, others staring into space, one or two crying. And Pop in tears. Lorna had never seen a man crying before. She slipped out of the room, feeling cold and sick inside.

It was like thinking you were safe, she thought, in a castle with walls and battlements and a drawbridge, and then somebody came along and knocked them all down and there you were in the middle without even a suit of armour. There were Wicked Things all round so you didn't know which way to turn. She ran up to her bedroom and curled up under the duvet in the dark, but the Wicked Things were still there.

It was better, though, by the time the Task Force came home. The excitement was terrific. They all sat round the television and watched as the grey-silver ships slid back into harbour with bands and balloons and coloured streamers. It was easy to laugh again with the families on the dockside waving their huge placards, and the children decked out in funny hats. Even the punks had dyed their hair red white and blue for the occasion. The fun was back and it seemed almost as if the part in the middle had never happened. It had all been a bad dream.

Phil came home four weeks later.

Pop had pulled into the layby at the top of the hill as usual. In the shimmering summer heat-haze the countryside lay before them, a spread of corn-gold fields as far as the eye could see, ripening in the sun. Amongst them the new airfield stood out an intense bright green ringed with scarlet poppies nodding in the long grass.

Lorna breathed in again the warm familiar smell of hot tarmac, grass, and aviation fuel, mingling with the leather of the old car seats. Pop struck a match and she caught a quick pungent whiff of burning phosphorus as he puffed slowly on his pipe.

Suddenly he stopped.

'He's back,' he said reaching for the ignition key. 'Phil's home again.'

The Spitfire swung into a Victory Roll and followed the old Jaguar down the track to the huts. Far off at the end of the runway, a small slim figure with ginger-blond hair stood alone.

Pop stopped the car and sat watching as Phil carefully brought the little plane round on a final circuit of the airfield; then landed it bouncing, on the cracked runway.

Lorna reached for the car door handle.

'He's out of practice. Even I could do better!'

Pop stretched across and put a hand over hers. She could feel he was shaking slightly.

'Just a minute lass,' he said. They sat and waited as Phil taxied the little plane up to where he stood. He bent and carefully laid the control unit on the ground, taking what seemed like an age. Then straightening up, he turned and waved.

Pop climbed out and walked across, with Lorna following.

'Good to see you, Phil,' he said quietly.

'Thanks. . . .' Phil paused. They stood looking at each other, the young blue eyes and the old grey ones. The silence stretched between them.

It was as if something was being said, thought Lorna, but she couldn't hear it. There was a different wave-band, one she couldn't tune into.

It was unbearable.

She turned away, blinking back tears and leaned against Phil's car. On the seat lay his cap and uniform jacket. There was an extra stripe on the sleeve.

'You're a Flight Lieutenant, that's *marvellous*! What happened? Come on, tell us, what did you do?'

Pop looked at Phil. Phil looked back, smiled and shrugged.

'Nothing much, just commandeered a couple of crates of Mars Bars for the boys.'

And that was all he would say.

QUARTET

1. The Winter Tree

Kevin leaned against the wall at the end of the playground and watched the boys from his class. Football was out on a morning like this so they were playing Headers, passing the ball around the ring. Now and then there was a shout as one of them missed and the ball landed with a soft squelch in the dirty slush.

Kevin had been one of the first to see the snow that morning. He had to leave home with his mum when she went to work and he had walked up the sparkling white empty playground backwards from the gate. From the school door it looked as if his feet had gone off on their own somewhere walking out across the new snow and vanishing into the city, lost among the cars and buses.

It was a nice thought, anyway.

Ten minutes. That was all it had taken to ruin the sheer white Arctic playground. Now it was spoiled and dirty, and nobody cared. They were all too busy with the football to notice.

It was simply a prison yard again, and a particularly messy one at that.

Football seemed to be the only thing that mattered at this new school. Kevin wasn't very good – never had been really – but he'd brought his own ball anyway on the off-chance of someone asking him for a game. Not likely! It seemed as if they'd all sorted themselves into teams in Primary One. There was no hope for a player with two left feet who had arrived into the middle of Primary Six like an alien from another planet.

The boys chased the ball round to the sheds, shouting and yelling. Kevin was left alone, hunched against the damp wall. It seemed the right place to be.

Nobody ever went near the Wall unless they had to. They told some daft stories about what lay on the other side. Some said it was a haunted house, others said there was an old woman who could put a spell on you. Jimmy Bell said he knew someone who had gone round collecting for Bob-a-Job week at the house and had never been seen since! No one seemed to know how the stories had started but the whole school was agreed about one thing – it was Bad Luck to play near the Wall. Jimmy Bell said the old witch sat up in a tree sometimes and watched them in the playground.

Jimmy . . . Jimmy . . . all you ever heard in Primary Six was Jimmy Bell. He was the greatest at everything – football included, of course.

Jimmy Bell organised all the action in Primary Six and if he didn't like you – too bad. He had tried to talk to Kevin that first day he started school.

'You're new. Miss Mackintosh told us about your dad. What happened to him?' Jimmy Bell's eyes were alight, waiting for the gory details.

'Push off,' said Kevin shoving past him and that was the end of the friendship. No chance of him ever fitting into Primary Six now.

Kevin slouched away from the Wall, threw his ball into the air and kicked. Usually he missed. This time, by some incredible fluke, he hit it one of those magic kicks that win the day at Hampden Park. The ball soared high against the grey sky, hung for a second – and then dropped neatly, on the other side of the Wall.

'That was a bit daft,' said a voice behind him – Margie Graham who sat in the back row of class and giggled a lot. 'How're you going to get it back?' Kevin shrugged.

'Shin over.' He tried for a foothold on the rough stone of the Wall and slipped back, skinning his hands.

'You can't go in *there*!' whispered Margie, her eyes like saucers. '*She'll* get you.'

Kevin ignored her and tried again. Margie stood and watched him slipping and sliding. She glanced quickly round the playground and then turned back, cupping her hands together.

'Here, I'll give you a leg up.'

Kevin hesitated.

'Go on. Get a move on!'

He stepped up and, reaching out, pulled himself to the top of the Wall, swung one leg over and looked down.

'What's it like?' hissed Margie. 'Can you see your ball?'

'It's incredible,' whispered Kevin, more to himself than her. He swung both legs over to jump down on the other side.

'Here, just a minute,' Margie shouted. 'I'm coming too. Give us a hand up.' She scrambled up to lie panting on the top of the wall beside him; then, catching her breath she looked down.

'Wow!'

Beneath them lay a sea of bushes. Some were great masses of thick green shining leaves. Others, their leaves long since gone, poked spiky fingers through clumps of snow. Here and there strange little stone figures, half hidden, smiled wickedly up at them from beneath thick fluffy white hats. The garden lay absolutely still and empty – the snow perfect and clean.

From the big grey house to the Wall where they sat there was not a footprint to be seen. Everything seemed to be black or white as if they had wandered into an old photograph.

Except for the ball.

In the middle of the white lawn, under the black spreading branches of an old tree, was the only touch of colour, the shining blood red of Kevin's football. He took a deep breath and slid down, landing softly in the garden.

'No – don't' . . .' whispered Margie. 'I don't like this. It's not right. . . .' But Kevin was already crouching under the bushes, pushing through to the lawn.

'All right, wait for me,' she hissed, almost landing on top of him. Together they crept under cover of the leaves towards the tree.

Nothing moved. The garden seemed to hold its breath. The big grey house with heavy curtains at the windows watched like a cat, through half-shut eyes.

'I'm *telling* you,' insisted Margie, pulling at his anorak. 'There *is* a witch. I bet she keeps some lunatic locked up in there who's really a Duke – only his family won't let him have the money and they pay her. . . .'

'Shut up!' You could tell Margie was best in the class at Writing but this was not the time for it.

'Wait here,' Kevin whispered and crept out across the open lawn to where the tree reached out, pointing accusing black fingers towards the intruders in the garden.

Hardly breathing, he sneaked up behind the trunk and reached out for the ball. The rough grey bark felt almost warm under his hand after the icy wall, like a living thing. Kevin ran his fingers down the patterns, feeling the rough and smooth edges.

'Oh, hurry up,' Margie wished silently. He seemed to be taking forever. If he didn't get a move on it would be too late. And then suddenly it was.

The back door slowly opened.

Margie vanished back under the bushes. Kevin froze by the tree, the red ball in his hands. There was no point in trying to run. Nowhere to hide, anyway.

An old lady stepped out very carefully on to the path, one hand holding firmly to the door-post, the other clutching a dishful of crusts for the birds.

'Here – you – laddie!' she called suddenly seeing

Kevin. 'What are you up to?' The voice was high and squeaky, like a rusty gate that hasn't been used for a long time. She edged slowly down the path towards him.

'What are you doing here, eh? Vandalising my garden I suppose. Well?'

Kevin stood, frozen to the spot, staring at her. Since she stepped out of the back door he had not moved. Under the bushes Margie felt the hair on the back of her neck rise. She swallowed hard.

'I knew it,' she thought. 'She's turned him to stone! It's true. She's a *real* witch.'

And then Kevin moved, and spoke.

'My ball went over the wall. . . .' he stammered. 'I came to get it back.' The old woman walked across the snowy lawn leaving a trail of long shambling footprints in the perfect snow. She stopped and stared down at him. Her eyes were dark, and grey like the sky.

'I'm sorry. . . .'

'Should be, too,' snapped the old lady. Then she looked at him with a curious twinkle in her eyes. 'Weren't you frightened? They say I'm a witch, don't they?'

'No. . . .' Kevin started to blurt out.

'Havers!' said the old lady. 'Course they do. I can hear them on the other side of the wall with their silly stories. Witch, indeed!' She gave a strange cackling laugh. Kevin stepped back and bumped into the tree.

'Mind what you're doing to Father!' she snapped again.

80

'Father?' he whispered. The others had been right. If she wasn't a witch, she was at least completely batty.

'It's all there is of him, you know,' she said leaning over Kevin and patting the tree trunk. 'We planted it when he didn't come back.' She stroked the tree as if it had been a pet cat or dog.

'Back from where?'

'Over there.' She waved a hand vaguely towards the world outside the wall. 'You know. Passchendale. The Trenches. First War. But you're too wee to know about that. He went to be a soldier and never came back. Don't know where he's buried, so Mother planted the tree just to have something to remember.'

Kevin stared up into the branches, black against the sky, reaching down around them like protecting arms. He nodded, tears springing to his eyes. Behind the tears, in his memory he saw again his own father, setting off on that last morning, uniform pressed, boots polished until you could see your face in them.

'See you soon!' he had shouted as he went.

But he wouldn't. Not ever. Kevin swallowed hard. The old lady looked at him sideways.

'It's a good tree,' she said patting the trunk. 'Needs someone to climb it, though. This house used to be full of children. My brothers and I had lots of friends and cousins. I think the garden misses them most. My father would have fair loved to see them climbing his tree.'

Kevin smiled. He couldn't help smiling at the

thought of the old lady perched up in the branches like an ancient woolly owl. She smiled back. Over the wall the school bell rang out, to mark the end of the break. In the bushes Margie stirred, and the leaves rustled.

'Got to go,' said Kevin reaching for the ball.

'Very well,' snapped the old lady. She turned and walked back up the path to the house.

'You can come back again, if you like,' she called from the doorstep. 'And bring your friend too!'

'Hmph!' sniffed Margie in the bushes. Kevin stood and stared up at the Father Tree.

It was like his mother's best ring, the one she hardly ever wore now. On her hand it was beautiful, but buried in cotton-wool in the box it seemed even more precious somehow. It was as if the soft whiteness made it shine all the brighter.

The Tree was like that. In the still, white, snow-covered garden the branches reaching down to him seemed to have a special magic of their own.

'I'll be back,' said Kevin quietly. And then he shouted it as he made a dash for the wall. 'I'll be back – soon.'

QUARTET

2. *The Spring Tree*

It was pandemonium when the four o'clock bell rang.

Everyone raced out, pushing and tumbling. If there had been a fire they couldn't have been out faster.

All except for Kevin.

He hung around the Primary Six cloakroom, re-packing his school bag and tying and re-tying his shoelaces until the others had gone, and the school was an empty shell echoing to the sound of the Janitor's electric polisher.

Margie was waiting for him behind the shed.

'You going over the top today?' she asked. He nodded.

'Can I come with you?'

'OK.' Kevin sneaked a look around. The playground was completely deserted.

'You go first,' he said leaning against the wall and making a cradle with his hands. Margie stepped up and climbed onto the top of the high wall behind the shed. Kevin tossed up her school bag first and then his. She dropped them with a soft thud on the other side and reached down to give him a hand up. He had learned how to scramble up that wall in the past few weeks.

Together they swung both legs across and jumped down beside the bags – into the garden. Margie rolled over giggling.

'Just like the S.A.S.' she whispered.

Kevin froze. He felt the sudden hot blinding tears at the back of his eyes and swallowed hard. That hadn't happened for a while.

'Shut up!' he growled turning away. But he knew what she meant all the same. There was always that small tingle of excitement when he climbed the wall.

He wondered if that was how his dad had felt when he went out on the patrols. Maybe it had been like that on the last patrol. Probably not. He and the others had been walking down a perfectly ordinary road. You wouldn't have expected anything to happen there. It looked just like the High Street, same shops, same people. Kevin had seen the street on the television news and still couldn't believe that his dad would never come back from there.

Suddenly he felt guilty. It had all happened so quickly, almost a year ago, and there were times when it seemed like a bad dream. There were even days now when he never thought about Dad at all. Sometimes it was hard even to remember his face or voice, and the smiling photographs seemed like a stranger in another world. He was fading like a ghost and Kevin actually went around at school being quite happy. He had made friends with a couple of the boys, although Margie was still the only one who knew about the garden.

Everything had been fine until she had said, 'Just

like the S.A.S.' . . . and then the whole thing had come flooding back again, choking him. It lay like a lead weight on top of his happiness at being back in the garden.

He hadn't been there for a week. It had poured solidly for days on end and the old lady had told them not to come when it was so wet. The weather was lifting at last, though, and when Kevin called in that morning on his way to school she had smiled and nodded, pleased to see him again.

'Aye,' she said, casting a weather-eye on the sky. 'Enough blue to make a sailor's waistcoat. Spring's really on its way now. The two of you can come round and give me a hand after school.'

So here they were. Kevin had been looking forward all day to the thought of working in the quiet garden. Somehow it felt more like home than the tiny flat he and Mum had moved to. And for him, too, the old lady's tree had become a part of the way he felt about his own dad. All winter it had stood black and dead and cold, just the way he felt inside now.

'I'm going home,' he said searching around for his bag. 'Tell her I couldn't come. . . .' But Margie wasn't listening.

'Kevin, Kevin! The Tree!' she shouted wriggling out from under the bushes. 'Come and see what's happened. Quick!'

Kevin dragged his bag out and brushed it down. The soft damp earth smelt fresh and different somehow from the way it had been for the last week or two. It was an exciting green sort of smell as if something was happening in the garden. He wiped his hands down his jeans and crawled out on to the grass.

Margie was gazing spellbound up into the branches of the tree. Kevin stared. He reached out and stroked the rough bark gently, shaking his head in wonder. All about him the network of spiky black twigs had exploded into a riot of pale pink and white flowers. Above them the pale spring sunlight filtered down through the mass of delicate petals.

'It's like a wedding dress,' shouted Margie, twirling round on the grass. A gust of wind shook the branches and a white shower of confetti petals fluttered around them.

'You've got some in your hair,' she giggled, reaching up to brush it off.

'You too!' Kevin and Margie laughed at each other.

The back door opened and the old lady came slowly down the path.

'Well, what do you think of that, then?' she said, as if she had done it all herself.

'Gorgeous,' shouted Margie dancing round the lawn, scattering handfuls of petals. 'Fantabulistic!' The old lady smiled at her.

''S' magic,' whispered Kevin.

'You know, I think it really is,' she said. 'I knew you'd like it. Never ceases to amaze me how it knows to do that every spring.' They stood together in silence, marvelling at the sight.

'Come on,' she said at last. 'Work to be done. Did you two find out how to prune those roses for me?'

'We did,' said Kevin. He and Margie had spent all Saturday afternoon in the library looking through gardening books until they found one on roses. They had read through all there was about pruning and cutting and Margie had copied that part out. Her handwriting was better.

The one thing Kevin did not want to do was take the book home. His mother would ask what he was up to because they didn't have a garden at the flat. He didn't really understand why, but he knew he didn't want to tell her about the old lady. Not just yet.

They knelt in the soft earth and Kevin showed the old lady how the buds were beginning to grow. It was just like the photographs in the book. He cut back the stem to just above a bud so that the rose would grow strong and firm, and explained why the cut had to slope away from the bud so that the rain water would not damage the growing flower. The old lady listened intently.

'My, but you're a clever laddie,' she said admiringly. Kevin felt his face become quite pink.

'Not as good as Margie. She always gets top marks for everything.'

'Aye, well that's clever too, right enough. But there's more things matter than top marks. You can be clever in ways they've never even thought about at that school of yours – and they're just as important.'

'My dad used to say something like that,' said Kevin, remembering a night they spent struggling with his Maths homework.

'Clever man, your dad,' said the old lady. 'Now let's get on with some work.'

They pottered quietly in the garden as the afternoon drew in. The wind suddenly grew colder and a shower of icy spring rain rattled down through the petals, driving them into the house.

'Time for a cup of tea before you go home,' said the old lady setting out the cups and saucers on a tray.

After they had finished and washed up they went back down the path for a last look at the Tree. The black clouds had cleared just as quickly as they came, leaving a world glittering with raindrops and strong with the smell of wet earth. High above them a rainbow stretched across the rooftops.

'It's over the school,' said Margie. 'Does that mean we'll find a pot of gold in the playground, d'you suppose?' They all laughed at that idea.

As they were leaving the old lady turned to Kevin.

'Would you like some of the blossom?' she said. 'I could cut a branch or two to take home to your mother.'

Kevin looked back at the tree, rich with the flowers of a new spring, the old dead twigs exploding with a new life.

He shook his head firmly.

'No, thanks,' he said. 'Leave them growing – just the way they are.'

QUARTET

3. The Summer Tree

'But Mum, why don't you come with me? The old lady would like to meet you.' It seemed like the hundredth time he had said it.

'I told you, Kevin. I don't want to go. . . .' His mum stopped and stood with her hands in the sink, staring out into the grey back court behind the tenement flat.

She sighed and rubbed hard at a collar she had already scrubbed three times since the argument started.

'Look,' she said quietly. 'I don't like . . . you know I don't like meeting new people . . . I don't want to . . . not since. . . .'

She couldn't even bear to talk about his dad or remember what had happened last year.

Kevin stamped out, kicking the kitchen door shut behind him. He flopped on to the chair in front of the television set and pressed through the buttons. It was the usual summer holiday rubbish, a series he remembered seeing when he was about seven and a cartoon programme that had been on at Christmas.

'Rubbish!'

'What's that?'

'Nothing.' He slammed the off button, picked up his anorak and looked round the kitchen door.

'I'm going for Margie,' he said. 'We told the old lady we'd be round this afternoon to cut her grass. . . . You're definitely not coming, then?' He knew it was useless but you had to keep trying. She couldn't stay in the flat forever, only going out to her part-time job in the office behind the builder's yard where she never spoke to anyone.

Margie reckoned his mum would go nuts if she went on like that. Margie was the only one who really knew about his mum and what had happened. She knew about the old lady and the garden over the Wall too, but she never told any of the others in class. Margie was good, she was someone you could trust and talk to.

But she wasn't there to talk to today.

'Sorry, Kevin,' said Margie's mum. 'Her cousins turned up out of the blue yesterday and she's gone off to stay with them for a few days.'

Kevin wandered down the road alone, idly kicking stones into the gutter. The school playground was completely deserted, the tarmac baking hot and sticky in patches. Round the back, in the shade by the Primary Seven classroom where he would be after the holidays, the painters were scraping the window frames. One of them was singing a pop song, very loudly and very badly to a transistor radio. The noise echoed along the empty corridors, mingling with the smell that could only be school. Jimmy Bell's gym shoes, disinfectant and chalk – even a faint whiff of school-dinner cabbage. All the new paint in the world would never get rid of that!

Over by the Wall Kevin looked round quickly. Nobody was watching. He pulled an empty dustbin out from behind the shed, climbed up and jumped down into the shade of the thick green bushes on the other side.

He could have walked round by the road and gone in the old lady's front gate of course, but it wouldn't be the same. The first time he had been in the garden he had climbed over with Margie and it still seemed as if that was the only way to go. It made the place feel more secret. Postmen, milkmen and paperboys used the front gate. Climbing the Wall made the garden his in some strange way.

Kevin crawled out from under the glossy leaves and looked around. The garden was still, peaceful and dazzling in the bright sunlight.

'Den!' he whispered. That was how it made him feel. It was the one safe place in the middle of a mad game, the place where nobody could touch you. He rolled over, smelling the fresh grass. The daisies were getting thick again, he would have to cut it but not just now. The old lady always had a rest in the afternoon between two and three o'clock, and her ancient motor mower would waken people three streets away, never mind in the house.

Kevin lay on his stomach squinting through the blades of grass. It was like a tiny jungle teeming with insect life. Under the surface the fat worms crawled back and forwards like the little orange subway trains in the city centre, round and round the lawn, in and out of the tree roots.

The Tree. When Kevin first discovered it, the Tree

had been black and dead. Spring had brought blossom and the promise of new life, and now with summer it was a parasol of pale green leaves sheltering the tiny apples that grew among them. Kevin stretched out, feeling the heat soaking into his back through the thin anorak and tee-shirt. He pulled a book from his pocket, scrambled to his feet and made for the shade of the Tree.

He climbed slowly and carefully, placing his feet gently on the old crusty branches until he came to the wide Y-shaped fork. It was here that he and Margie sat, inside the cool green canopy with the light flickering on the pages, to read the book. He would have to finish it himself now, and within seconds he was deep in the story of pirates, treasure and the 'Hispaniola' her sails filling to the wind, dipping through the blue seas to a tropic shore. The sun moved round slowly, birds and butterflies came and went among the branches, but Kevin read on, lost in the green and gold swaying world about him.

Coming at last to the end of a chapter he looked up. Three o'clock had long since come and gone, and there was no sign of the old lady. Perhaps in this heat she had slept longer than usual. He wrapped the book in his anorak and slid down the tree. She was nowhere in the garden.

Kevin knocked on the back door, but the house sounded hollow and empty. Through the kitchen window he could see the tea tray with the cups and fruit cake left ready for them. Kevin hesitated, then tried the back-door knob.

'Hello!' he called uncertainly. 'It's me, Kevin.'

There was no answer. In the hall her coat still hung on the hook and the old straw hat and bag sat neatly side by side on the table under the mirror – as they always did when she was in.

Kevin felt a sudden kick of fear in his stomach. Not here – not in this beautiful place. Surely nothing could go wrong here. He searched from room to room downstairs. Everywhere the quiet polished furniture reflected his movements. The image of his thin white face flitted through shining mirrors, held for a second and then passed on. The tall ticking clock in the hall seemed to grow louder and louder in his head.

He found her at last, upstairs, lying on the floor by the bed.

'Kevin,' she whispered. 'I was dizzy getting up. I . . . fell. . . .' He knelt, hardly daring to touch her. Should she be moved? Maybe that was the wrong thing to do.

'Wait here!' he shouted and ran. Stupid thing to say, he thought as he pounded along the road to the builder's yard. Where was she going to go, anyway?

'Hey!' the man in the yard yelled after him. Kevin ignored him and tumbled, panting, into the office where his mother worked.

'She's had an accident. . . .' he gasped, fighting for breath. 'The old lady's fallen. You've *got* to come.' His mother looked up, saw his face and grabbed her jacket and bag.

'Just a minute – you run on,' she shouted, turning back to 'phone for an ambulance. They raced down the road and were there five minutes before it.

Kevin's mum held the old lady's hand as they waited.

'You'll be all right,' she said. 'Don't worry about anything. Kevin and me, we'll keep an eye on the house. We'll come and see you in hospital, too, and make sure you're all right. Everything'll be fine, you'll see.'

Kevin stared at her. It was the first time in months she had offered to go anywhere that wasn't work, or the supermarket.

He caught his breath and found he was crying. The old lady patted his hand.

'Don't worry, Kevin. I'm not that bad. I'm not away yet awhile.' Kevin smiled and shook his head.

It didn't really matter that she thought he was crying for her. It didn't matter at all.

He stood at the bedroom window, looking down onto the shimmering green tree through his tears, the tree that had been planted for the old lady's father who went to war and never came home again, just like his own.

His mother came over and put an arm round him.

'Dad would have been awful proud of you today,' she said at last. It was the first time she had spoken about him in months.

'Thank you,' he whispered. But whether it was to the tree or to his mother, he wasn't quite sure.

QUARTET

4. The Autumn Tree

Kevin could hardly believe his ears. In the six years he had been at primary school nobody had ever said he was really good at anything. But here he was, right at the beginning of Primary Seven, and Miss MacLean his new teacher, had just said the magic words.

'It's very good, Kevin. Definitely the best in the class. I think you should read it out to the others.'

Margie, sitting behind him, poked his back and whispered, 'Cleverclogs!' She was usually best at writing, but Kevin knew she was as pleased as him. He went out to the front of the room, took his paper from Miss MacLean and looked around.

Two days back after the holidays and everyone was still neat and clean in new clothes. They weren't at all like the same crowd who had rushed around the playground kicking a ball and completely ignoring him when he had arrived as a new boy just after the Christmas holidays. It was funny, he thought, they all looked new now with their tidy haircuts and shining shoes. He wasn't the different one any more.

'Go on, Kevin,' encouraged Miss MacLean. He started to read.

'What I did during the Summer Holidays. . . .'

He went on to tell the story of how he had visited old Mrs Campbell's garden, how he had first found it when he climbed over the Wall from the School. He told the story about the Tree the old lady's family had planted for her father who never came home from the First War. He told about the day he had found the old lady lying in the bedroom and how he and his mum had gone to hospital with her in the ambulance and how they visited her regularly now that she was home again.

'And I think we should always visit old people,' he finished, 'because they are just like everyone else, except they are lonely. They like to have someone to talk to, and besides their stories are really interesting, sometimes.'

He folded the piece of paper and sat down, his face quite pink. Now everyone knew about Mrs Campbell and the Tree and his mum. He hadn't really meant that to happen.

Miss MacLean smiled again and looked round the class.

'I wonder how many of you visit old people regularly.'

'Please, Miss, we visit my gran on Sundays,' said Margie. 'She always gives us sweets but my mum says they're not good for your teeth.'

'My grandad let me taste his beer once. . . .' Jimmy Bell chipped in. It started a discussion that went on until the bell rang for break. As they tumbled out into the corridor the others crowded round Kevin.

'She's not really a witch, then?'

'Isn't the garden haunted at all?'

'Och, that's a swizz. . . .' Kevin laughed and shook his head.

'Coming for a game of football?' said Jimmy Bell grabbing his arm. Miss MacLean followed them out.

'I'd like to meet your old lady, Kevin,' she said. 'Could you take me with you sometime soon, do you think?'

'Come today,' said Kevin. 'It'll be all right. Mum's taking some baking round at four o'clock and I'm meeting her there. You could come and have tea with us.'

'I'd like that. We'll go round at four, then.' As Kevin dashed out into the playground she called after him.

'Can we go round by the gate, please? I don't fancy shinning over the wall in these shoes!'

'Right!' Kevin ran out still laughing at the idea of little round Miss MacLean in her dangly earrings and long skirt trying to climb over into the garden. He always climbed the Wall himself but just this once he would go round by the road.

Tea was already set in the front room by the fire. They usually had it in the garden.

'That's a right snell wind getting up this afternoon,' said the old lady, passing round the cups. 'Autumn's not far off.'

After tea Kevin wandered out into the garden. The wind-tossed branches of the tree dipped and swayed, and here and there an apple lay in the long grass around the trunk.

He stood under the green parasol listening to the swish of the leaves. There was more daylight shining through them now, and the little round apples were bigger, and turning from green to a soft orange red. The old lady had said they would be ready for picking soon. Kevin watched them bouncing in the wind, hanging on tightly to their twigs.

'Why don't they just fall off?' he had asked.

'They're like folks, I suppose,' said the old lady. 'They'll hang on to what they know until they're ready to let go.'

The apples were still hanging on tightly.

'You coming home tonight?' his mum called from the house. Kevin patted the rough grey bark.

'Bye,' he whispered and hurried back across the lawn.

'Miss MacLean wondered if you'd like all the class to come round and pick the apples on Saturday,' said Mum on their way home. 'You could all help to make them into jelly.'

Kevin felt a thump of panic inside. He stuffed his fists in his pockets. He hated the idea of lots of people sharing his garden, his Tree, the place where he came to be alone.

'Mrs Campbell thinks it's a very good idea,' said his mum.

Kevin said nothing. He was thinking. He was thinking back to the first time he had climbed into the garden on a cold winter day when the Tree stood stark and black against the white snow.

'This house used to be full of children,' the old

lady had said. 'My brothers and I had lots of friends and cousins. I think the garden misses them. My father would have loved to see them all climbing his tree. . . .'

Kevin thought of his own father. He would have loved the garden. He would have organised everyone into working parties to pick and sort the apples and ordered them about like a daft Sergeant Major.

It would have been so much fun the thought hurt.

'What about it?' said Mum softly. 'Miss MacLean will get everyone to bring some empty jars and sugar. I'll come too and help you all make the jelly. It'll be great, you'll see. . . .'

'OK,' said Kevin. 'Yes . . . all right.'

Saturday morning dawned fresh and clear and windy. By nine o'clock the garden was full of Kevin's class climbing trees, playing cops and robbers in the bushes or just exploring.

Some of them were even picking apples.

Miss MacLean turned up on the back of a huge black motorbike. Primary Seven were pop-eyed with amazement! Miss MacLean wore jeans and a huge woolly sweater with a rainbow across the front. Miss MacLean was hanging on tightly to a huge young man with a curly beard who called her Sandy!

'That's her boyfriend Dave,' whispered Margie. 'He's *gorgeous*.' Kevin shrugged.

'Nice motorbike,' he said.

Dave organised everyone, he was all over the garden at once, chivvying them along and cracking jokes until even Kevin had to laugh. By lunchtime all the apples were piled in boxes, baskets and bags in the kitchen.

'Clock off!' shouted Dave and they had a quick break swopping sandwiches, crisps and corny jokes with Miss MacLean, Dave and Kevin's mum. The old lady sat and listened and laughed.

'Right, back to work, you lot,' said Kevin's mum at last. 'Jelly time!'

Hours later Kevin wandered out of the warm, sticky, sweet-smelling kitchen. The afternoon sky shaded to a soft green-blue above the Tree. The leaves were already turning from green to gold in the autumn sunshine. Some of them, caught by a sudden sharp gust of wind, fluttered around him as he stood alone.

Suddenly, Kevin remembered seeing on television poppy petals fluttering down on old men who had fought with Mrs Campbell's father in the First War. They settled too, on the shoulders and shining boots of the young men who had fought in the same army as his own father. He heard again the words ringing round the arena:

'They shall grow not old, as we that are left grow old. . . .'

He watched the tumbling yellow leaves float down to the grass and knew then that the Tree would grow again, green and fresh, next spring.

Behind him, there was a short burst of laughter from the kitchen as the door opened and closed again. The old lady came down the path still

106

smiling, her cheeks rosy from the heat of the cooker. She stopped by his side and stood looking up at her father's Tree.

'The others wondered where you'd got to,' she said at last. 'Are you coming back to join us?'

'Yes. Yes of course,' Kevin smiled, and together they walked back up the path to the noisy bright kitchen, leaving the Tree to drop its golden leaves in the quiet garden.

Long years past, walking so fast,
Bravely they marched away.
Cannon roared loud, and in the mad crowd,
Wounded and dying lay.
Up goes a shout, a horse dashes out,
Out from the ranks so blue,
Gallops away to where Joe lay,
Then came the voice he knew.

'Did you think I would leave you dying
When there's room on my horse for two?
Climb up here, Joe, we'll soon be flying.
I can go just as fast with two.

Did you say, Joe, I'm all a-tremble?
Perhaps it's the battle's noise.
But I think it's that I remember,
When we were two little boys.'

MAN IN MOTION
Jan Mark

Once Lloyd has started at his new school, he soon finds he's playing cricket with Salman, swimming with Kenneth, cycling with James and playing badminton with Vlad. But American football is Lloyd's greatest enthusiasm. And in time it tests his loyalties, not only to his other sporting activities, but also to the new friends he shares them with.

THE OUTSIDE CHILD
Nina Bawden

Imagine suddenly discovering you have a step-brother and -sister no one has ever told you about! It's the most exciting thing that's ever happened to Jane, and she can't wait to meet them. Perhaps at last she will become part of a 'proper' family, instead of forever being the outside child. So begins a long search for her brother and sister, but when she finally does track them down, Jane finds there are still more surprises in store!

THE FOX OF SKELLAND
Rachel Dixon

Samantha's never liked the old custom of Foxing Day – the fox costume especially gives her the creeps. So when Jason and Rib, children of the new publicans at The Fox and Lady, find the costume and Jason wears it to the fancy-dress disco, she's sure something awful will happen.

Then Sam's old friend Joseph sees the ghost of the Lady and her fox. Has she really come back to exact vengeance on the village? Or has her appearance got something to do with the spate of burglaries in the area?

FLOWER OF JET

Bell Mooney

It's the time of the miners' strike. Tom Farrell's father is branded with the word Tom most dreads; Melanie Wall's father is the strike leader. How can Tom and Melanie's friendship survive the violence and bitterness of both sides? Things are to grow far worse than they ever imagined, for Melanie and Tom discover a treacherous plot that could destroy both their families. And they have to act fast if they're going to stop it.

MIGHTIER THAN THE SWORD

Clare Bevan

Adam had always felt he was somehow special, different from the rest of the family, but could he really be a modern-day King Arthur, the legendary figure they're learning about at school? Inspired by the stories they are hearing in class, Adam and his friends become absorbed in a complex game of knights and good deeds. All they need is a worthy cause for which to fight. So when they discover that the local pond is under threat, Adam's knights are ready to join battle with the developers.

Reality and legend begin to blur in this lively, original story about an imaginative boy who doesn't let a mere wheelchair stand in his way of adventure.

AGAINST THE STORM

Gaye Hicyilmaz

'As Mehmet is drawn into his parents' ill-considered scheme to go and live in Ankara, the directness and the acute observation of Gaye Hicyilmaz carry the reader with him ... Terrible things happen: illness, humiliation, death. But Mehmet is a survivor, and as the book closes, "a sort of justice" has been done, and a satisfying victory achieved. It is a sort of justice too ... that in all the dire traffic of unpublishable manuscripts something as fresh and powerful as this should emerge' – *The Times*